The *FIVE*

"Ps"

FOR TEENS

The *FIVE*
" P s "
For Teens

Copyright © 2011 by John A. Andrews.

Published in the U.S.A. by
BooksThatWillEnhanceYourLife.com

A L I
Andrews Leadership International
www.AndrewsLeadershipInternational.com

ISBN: 9780983141983
Cover Design: ALI
Cover Photo: Anthony Johnson
Cover Graphics: Abhai Kaul
Edited by: Teen Success

This book is dedicated to my three sons, Jonathan 15, Jefferri 13 and Jamison 12. The trio has filled my life with drive and purpose, thereby enhancing my entire scope for the future. YOU keep me blazing the trails… I love YOU and I am proud of YOU!

-Dad.

Table of Contents

AUTHOR'S PREFACE

I'm writing this book for *teens* because:

1. I have two teenage sons and another soon to enter adolescence, and want all teens to be given the information/tools necessary to become successful.
2. I'm passionately embarking on a significant adventure; looking for teenagers who are willing to dare "walls" getting in the way of their vocation.
3. Our world needs young adults, who are willing to step off the sidelines and into the game – making a difference, to be successful and contributing citizens in the world.

I've discovered that most people in their early twenties to mid thirties don't really know what they want – they are dreamless. Evidently they have lived some of their greatest years without laying the proper foundation that will/can lead them to creating massive success in life.

In addition, several women in their late twenties have told me that it's hard finding a guy in his thirties who possess a success mindset and philosophy. They want a guy who can solve problems because in life whether you like it or not, you are going through a problem, embarking on a problem, or wrapping up a problem. That's the way it is! This decline of a prepared generation has led me to believe that somewhere our society has dropped the ball. Yes, when it comes to preparing our youngsters for massive success and if it's not picked up soon enough - future generations could wind up immersed in that deficit.

I read my first book on personal development *The Magic of Thinking Big* almost 25 years ago when I was---. I'll tell you it has made a significance difference in my whole mindset and philosophy - when it comes to setting and reaching goals. That book taught me: 1) The power of believing in possibilities – faith can remove mountains. 2) The people who fail in life are bent on making excuses as to why they can't succeed. 3) Action will cure any fear.

In January 2011 after speaking on the 4 "Ps" at Martin Luther King Jr. Day celebrations in Eugene, Oregon, I visited Honolulu, Hawaii. I had never been to Hawaii, and was stoked to be there signing my National Bestseller *Rude Buay ... The Unstoppable* for Barnes and Noble. I decided to stay in China Town and as a result made connections with the YMCA Youth Department. I was invited to address their teens on success. After speaking on the 4 "Ps" based on my book *Dare To Make A Difference Success 101 for Teens,* I opened up the floor for some questions. An Asian teen, who wanted to know more about me than any of his peers asked if I was planning on adding another "P" to the "4 Ps". So now you have it: The *FIVE* "Ps" For Teens.

Embarking on my quest, I'm daring you to think outside of the box, act outside of the box, dream outside of the box and the legacy you'll pass on will be one remembered for generations to come. Your grand children and great grand children will never forget your name.

-   JOHN A. ANDREWS

The FIVE "Ps" For Teens

Our deepest fear is not that we are inadequate.
Our deepest fear is that we are powerful beyond measure.
It is our light, not our darkness that most frightens us.

We ask ourselves, who am I to be brilliant, gorgeous, talented and fabulous?
Actually, who are you not to be?
You are a child of god. Your playing small doesn't serve the world.

There's nothing enlightened about shrinking so that other people won't feel insecure around you.
We were born to make manifest the glory of God that is within us.
It's not just in some of us, it's in everyone.

And, as we let our own light shine, we unconsciously give other people permission to do the same. As we are liberated from our own fear, our presence automatically liberates others.[1]

- Marianne Williamson

x

INTRODUCTION

Like the caterpillar going through the cocoon to become a beautiful butterfly, equally, all truly successful people go through walls, which stood in their way towards their destiny. They will also tell you that their success principles were rooted deep inside of them and were the defining agents which helped create the success that you see all around them. If you nurture those roots which run deep within you, your chance of succeeding is inevitable.

Most kids already know who they want to become way before the age of five, and they are not afraid to tell you. To them it's never like a broken record and they repeat it every chance they get. Ask any pre-teen what they want to become when they grow up and they'll confidently respond as that destiny was given to them at birth. You hear it repetitively you'll never ever forget it. With their limited experiences of failure they never surrender to "walls" real or imagined en-route to their accomplishing their desire. They just know that they want it and want it so badly that succeeding seems

inevitable. They aren't tentative when it comes to launching out into the unknown.

Making their first step is a classic example. That child would first find an object to support his stance, and then set himself free while maintaining his balance. Suddenly off he goes with that first unsupported step. Even if he falls flat on his face, he gets up and tries again. If he doesn't succeed he tries it again the following day until his mission is accomplished. At such a tender age he understands that if he falls off the horse he must get back on if he's ever going to walk.

I'm always amazed by such genius in kids and their nothing is impossible mindset. However, as these same kids become adults, conditioned by their environment to fail - their goals and dreams suddenly look unreachable. They sometimes let dream stealers question their abilities as well as their ideas. Unintentionally or maliciously (they-use) others inject them with venom, killing their dreams along with their desire to accomplish great things.

Many people, failing to discover themselves go to their grave with their music still unleashed. We mourn their death – a great lose. Conversely we overlook the fact that the greatest lose is what died in many of us while we are yet still alive. The King of Pop, Michael Jackson, though experiencing a problematic lifestyle during the years leading up to his death, seemed to be one of the few entertainers of our time who didn't take his music to the grave with him – he certainly *didn't stop til he got enough* and his music was *off the wall*.

I was born in the beautiful islands of St. Vincent and the Grenadines. And came from a family of eight siblings, although my parents gave birth to eleven, the other two I'd never met. They passed on at an early age. I have five sisters and three brothers and I came in at number eight. Not sure if that number made me the odd ball.

My dad was a carpenter and passed on when I was only nine. Mom was a factory owner. She was confronted with opportunities to remarry during those tough times which followed. Mom turned them all down, stating that her obligations were to the nine of us. She fought through the tough times, not even able to afford me shoes to wear to school. My church shoes were mostly pre-owned and passed down from my elder brother who earned his own wages. I made it a habit of refurbishing them myself. Even if they were too big for my feet I stuffed them with news paper to make them fit. My first new pair of good shoes came a few years before going to high school. They were black leather and fitted comfortably. Before then, my mother bought me a pair of very inexpensive shoes made of rubber – an enemy to the scorching hot sun where I lived.

I was a tough kid bent on doing things my way. The words "John you seem to have a stick broken in your ears" meaning that *"I'm bent on doing things my way no matter what they said"*. That statement meant very little to me back then. The phrase, like a broken record was heard constantly from my parents and older siblings alike. So much that I became familiar to the "rod" and they certainly didn't spoil me.

Nevertheless I was tops in my class, got straight A's in just about every subject. I read, and read some more every opportunity I got and studied hard. I made up in activity what I lacked in talent. My small clique of school friends were of the same aptitude though more talented than I was. Running with the ambitious started for me back in my teens and has always remained my mindset and philosophy.

I finished Belmont School at top of my class. I followed that up by excelling in my "(common entrance exams)" the equivalent of the GED exam in the United States. This allowed me to not only enroll at Mountain View Academy, a Christian High School of mom's religion. But, allowed me to skip the first class. My eldest sister was so proud of me she eagerly picked up my tuition for the first two years. A religious school? It was apparent at least what our family envisioned for me. They no doubt saw me probably heading up a church after graduation. They had seen me put benches together, erect a podium and minister to an empty room on numerous occasions.

Mom continued where my sister left off and with some of her meager resources saw me through most of that religious high school. She struggled trying to make ends meet with nine mouths to feed plus hers. I remembered her saying at one point: "John, this is all I can afford." Consequently I dropped out of high school and resorted to learning auto body repairs. If nothing else I did learn a whole lot about discipline and great examples of *faith* from the bible while at the academy. I was so intrigued by the story of Job and his ability to pursue even after he lost all that he had.

My teenage years were molded on strong relationship values – my mom saw to it that they were. She dragged my eight siblings and me to church weekly. She said we had to attend if we lived under her roof. Even if our worship attire had to be recycled, she insisted on our involvement. She talked with other church members about our potential. Mom was very proud of us and of the seeds being sown within us. It didn't matter to her that the weekly two-mile walks each way contributed to wearing out our church shoes. She viewed the process as a by-product of developing fortitude in us.

Mom served as my first personal development coach. Back then she would say, very philosophically: "What you give out in your right hand you're going to receive in your left. You can do whatever you set in your heart and mind to accomplish. If you can think it, you can do it." For a while, I thought she was too immersed in the bible. But some of it did resonate in my delicate mind. One day she told me a story about a woman who went to the river every day, sit down on a huge stone with the soap and laundry next to her, and pray to God that he'd send her help to wash the daily-increasing load. But help never came. She might have had faith, but she wasn't willing to do the work, and help never came.

What are you willing to do with the gifts and abilities you've been endowed with? Is your dare strong enough to cause you to swim upstream when others around you are content to float downstream? The misfits in life are always known to have settled for far less than their best.

I've seen so many "would be greats" who sit on their talent. They have no zest, vim, vitality, passion or sense of purpose. Nothing drives them. They are like a train without a caboose. And they wonder why others are moving ahead in life while they're not. They're waiting for someone to inject them with a dose of success or, like the woman with the laundry, praying that God will bless their idle deeds.

Despite mom's vision for me becoming a pastor, I was obsessed with becoming a police officer when I grew up. So I studied policemen and even prayed to God that someday I would become one. So much that, several of my dreams and nightmares brought the vocation closer to my heart and soul. Would that be my profession? Circumstances changed after coming to America but the deep rooted passion has benefited me tremendously enabling me to write screenplays dealing with law enforcement. There's a famous goal setting quote, "If you shoot for the stars you could end up hitting the trees." How could you miss when you're shooting that high? My peers today know that I'm not only a visionary but much of an enforcer – one who delights in solving problems. I'm thankful that I had such vision and focus as a child, and developed myself in other areas of greatness as well. I like to see myself as an evolving human being, never like a tomato that's ripened but always on the cutting edge.

In 2009 Senator Barack Obama was elected as Americas' first black president. Obama, who rose to great success, grew up during the civil rights revolution of the 1960s, when blacks were not even permitted to ride in the front of the bus as whites did, dine in certain restaurants or even permitted to vote. In those days "segregation" was not only an academic institutional slogan, but rather an uncomfortable household word to the negro race. Bottom line: back then severe limits were placed on the associations of these two races - with blacks at a stringent disadvantage. Obama went through those walls and consequently earned the American vote.

During that civil rights era of intense racial conflicts, leaders such as Malcolm X and Dr. Martin Luther King Jr. emerged on the scene. King, a black man from the south fought for, and lost his life (assassinated) daring to fulfill his dream of equality. A dream that:

> One day his children would not be judged by the color of their skin but by the content of their character.[2] In addition: *that one day all children regardless of the color of their skin would live together in unity.* [3]

In 1969 a school teacher by day and an insurance agent by night from Oklahoma City, Harland Stonecipher, was involved in a head on collision automobile accident. His car got totaled as a result. The police officer called to the scene cited the other driver, a woman, at fault who then turned around and sued Harland Stonecipher. He was not only hospitalized but he exhausted his life savings of almost $4,000.00 defending himself against that lawsuit. He ended up winning but felt as though he had lost. In today's economy that sum would equal almost $40,000.00.

Consequently, Harland searched not only the U.S but also Europe and found out that most Europeans owned a legal plan in order to protect their rights. He adopted the concept and brought it to America, and now almost two million families have access to top quality advice whenever they need it for just over a dollar a day. Because of this adversity his destiny now embodies a two-fold mission. (1) To provide equal justice under law for all North American families. (2)To create more millionaires than any other company has ever created in history.[3]

Oprah Winfrey, although born in poverty and a victim of abuse and a troubled youth, rose to become by far the most powerful woman of our time. Oprah spent the kindergarten stage of her life living with her grandmother, who provided her with a strong disciplinary environment in which the church played a vital role.

One day Oprah stunned church members by delivering a reading and interpretation of a passage from the bible. Her grandmother taught her how to read and those skills were later honed by her grandfather. She was required to read books and, every two weeks, to write a report about what she had read. Oprah would often say that she wanted to make her living by talking. It was said that she became a gifted and quick-witted speaker. She knew way back then what she wanted to become, even though she grew up during the civil rights revolution when segregation was prevalent.

In 1972 she became the first black woman to hold the anchor position at Nashville's WTVF-TV. In 1986 she launched the Oprah Winfrey Show. In 1994 she bought her own studio "Harpo." In 1996 she began Oprah's book club to promote reading, for which she recommends a recently published book each month. She sets aside one show each month for a full discussion on the book. She has since created her classic book club which features 3 authors per year. Oprah habitually gives 10% of her income to charities, mostly having to do with youths, education and books.[4]

Oprah Winfrey, who became a billionaire at age 49, has not only risen to become the most powerful and influential woman in television but ruler of a large entertainment and communications empire - from a life of poverty and abuse to one of greatness. Oprah at one point in her broadcast career believed in herself so much, sources close to her knew that she was like a hit record to be released. It wasn't long before she became that hit record. She has broken down so many walls. Now when she talks - people absolutely listen. Today, Oprah Winfrey not only owns her a Television Network but calls it OWN – Oprah Winfrey Network.

Is your destiny one of greatness – a cause greater than self? There are things you and I will accomplish in our lifetime that will not only astonish our relatives, friends, neighbors, co-workers but our enemies alike. But first we must understand the value of our untapped potential. It has been discovered that 90% of an iceberg rests beneath the surface. It may surprise you that each of us has at least 90% of our potential lying untapped. As human beings we are known to only use that other 10% of our potential.

In my interaction with successful people from all walks of life, I've discovered that they are not only specialists in their field but that they had at one point in their lives said yes to their potential. In my journey up the ladder of success, I've learned to become as "a sponge" by learning from them. I've worn their shoes, and felt some of their pain. You will meet most of them through these pages as you will me. Most of all because success leaves clues, you will discover that they recognized their value, believed in their value, increased their value, and consequently they've become valuable. Additionally, you would realize that they tapped into their potential, developed passion, and purpose, enhanced their personality and harnessed the power of persistency.

Our world has been searching for you. It needs people who are willing to step off the sidelines and into the game - willing to make a significant difference. These *FIVE* "Ps" are designed for YOU.

"I DARE YOU TO ACHIEVE SOMETHING THAT WILL MAKE THE FUTURE POINT TO YOU WITH EVEN MORE PRIDE THAN THE PRESENT IS POINTING TO THOSE WHO HAVE GONE BEFORE YOU."

\- WILLIAM DANFORTH

P 1

POTENTIAL

In his book, *The Genius Machine,* author Gerald Sindell asks:

> "How can you get out of your own ocean to see what differentiates you?"[2]

Based on the worlds populous of almost seven billion people, you stand out. You might reason – Really? Me? No Way! That's impossible. I am nobody. I don't have the brains. I am from the wrong side of the tracks. I don't have what it takes I am not the best tool in the shed. I am not, I am not, and I am not. If you are holding onto those false beliefs about yourself – Understand, they are nothing but figments of your imagination. Those shackles, once removed, put you in the drivers' seat, allowing you to become the best YOU. In life you will stand out.

Think about the last time you were looking at a collection of pictures. Did you find yourself looking for you, even when you knew you weren't in the picture? It's our human tendency to look first to see if we are included because it's all about what's in it for me or where do I fit into the scheme of things. Also, if you were to, with time permitting, check out the entire world's population, you won't find anyone exactly like you, including anyone with your particular abilities, intelligence or viewpoint. Have you ever pondered and come to the realization that there's a reason why you are the only one with your voice, thumb print along with many other attributes?

What if I was to tell you that you have the power within you to become successful? That you have in this moment, a power which lays dormant, like a volcano. When discovered and tapped into, will erupt and lift you from failure to success. This power can assist you in transforming into a person who can experience tremendous influence and success. I know this may be hard to believe, comprehend or figure out – based upon your life experiences.

What if I were to tell you is that all you have to do is to trust your power by *knowing yourself*? In his book *On Becoming a Leader* Warren Bennis writes,

"Know thyself, then, means separating who you are and who you want to be from what the world thinks you are and wants you to be."[2]

It is often said that KNOWLEDGE IS POWER. Self knowledge is your first key to success. What I really want you to know is that if you really, I MEAN REALLY, REALLY know yourself, you'd understand that the sky is the limit to your potential! Knowing that alone would keep you up at night, unable to go to sleep, so excited about what can be! You'd be so captivated by such a burning desire to tap into and unleash your 90% unused potential. You'd be wide awake, planning the next series of moves for your life.

What are you willing to do to live your full potential?

➤ Are you willing to believe in yourself?

➤ Are you willing to incorporate new habits?

➤ Are you willing to associate with those who have your best in mind?

➤ Are you willing to develop a sense of passion. and purpose towards fulfilling your destiny?

➤ Would you, in exchange for a better, fuller and richer life step up to the plate?

YOU must realize that you're different. You are unique. You are beauty-fully and wonder-fully made. You are here, right now, and no one can be you but you. Be excitingly thankful and appreciative for who you are as well as who you can become. That's the power of tapping your potential.

Unfortunately and tragically, as human beings we place very little value on ourselves and subsequently acclimatize toward failure. We live in a world bombarded with negative news, pessimism and a mediocrity mindset. As a result, devaluing ourselves has become such an easy thing to do. Watching constant negative news for a few hours over a period of time and we are hooked, immersed in all that negativity. As the saying goes, "Garbage in garbage out." We hear and watch so much violence, now we're even afraid to go outside. Not only that, we've not only become fearful of others but also we fear our own potential resulting in living our life hiding our light from not only ourselves, but the world. The following is one of my favorite readings by Marianne Williamson:

> *Our deepest fear is not that we are inadequate.*
> *Our deepest fear is that we are powerful beyond measure.*
> *It is our light, not our darkness that most frightens us.*

We ask ourselves, who am I to be brilliant, gorgeous, talented and fabulous?
Actually, who are you not to be?
You are a child of god. Your playing small doesn't serve the world.

There's nothing enlightened about shrinking so that other people won't feel insecure around you.
We were born to make manifest the glory of God that is within us.
It's not just in some of us, it's in everyone.

And, as we let our own light shine, we un-consciously give other people permission to do the same. As we are liberated from our own fear, our presence automatically liberates others. [1]

Growing up as I kid I was always laughed at, called names such as ugly and skinny. None of those fit with who I am today. As a result, my self image was negatively impacted. Even if my mom instilled positive reinforcement, because my association with my classmates lasted much longer than the time I'd spent with her - I became negatively affected.

As an adult I've had to read many books on personal development in order to dilute those toxins and rediscover who I really am and could become. Today those names have become nothing but water under a bridge because I've constantly and consistently worked on myself.

As a responsible teenager on your way to the top, realize that you are always looking at two different walls. You'll find that one says you are top notch and you can do whatever you can think, want or desire. You have all the resources and support to make things happen. You were born to succeed. Nothing can stop you. Everything you touch turns to gold. Your unlimited potential will propel you to the top in your chosen vocation. You are enough. OWN it!

The other wall says: You grew up on the wrong side of the tracks, you can't do anything right. You will never have what you want. You have no capital or other resources and no one believes in you. You never follow through and finish things. You fail at everything you do. You don't have the right education and training. You are TOO---EVERYTHING!

Conversely, when it comes down to making a difference, everything starts with you. Once you really launch out, you'll discover if bent on success that:

> You are in the driver's seat.
> You call the shots.
> You are the captain of your own ship.

> ➢ You are the pilot of your own aircraft.
> ➢ You set your own pace.

Most of all, you are the only wall you must encounter towards your destiny. You chose success or failure. The ball is in your hands – you dribble or you shoot.

An individual focused on success must eliminate the blame game completely from one's mindset in order to have *true* success. If indulged, it becomes obvious that when pointing a finger at someone else, *there are three pointing back at them*. Instead, whenever the chips are down, they "saddle up" and focus on their destiny. In doing so one develops the morale that "It's all or nothing." He/She eats, breathes and lives success creating war on any "habit" which has kept or will keep one captive. With such a mindset in place, stepping out of one's comfort zone becomes an embracing challenge. Consequently, this move most likely results in a much richer and rewarding lifestyle. In my book *When the Dust Settles* I refer to the story about the baby elephant chained to a stake, and after several years, later, with the chain removed from its feet, the elephant refused from setting itself free. It didn't know what or how to be due to its longtime conditioning. To the elephant, the chain was still there.

How are you *chained* to you circumstances?

Living such a life chained to your circumstances is a chain you must break if your advancing is going to be inevitable.

Breaking yourself free and being all you can be will take some effort on your part. Similarly success is a choice, path taken purposefully and filled with both challenges and learning opportunities. I'm always reminded of the story of two men waiting at the dock.

> One man looked like he had been waiting there forever, putrid and unkept. A ship pulled up, dropped anchor and the agile man, while boarding said, "Good to see you again, pal." Then he jumped aboard the ship. Before setting sail he asked the waiting man: "What are you waiting for pal? I see you here all the time..." The waiting man responded: "My ship, of course." The man on the moving ship retorted, "Did you send one out? "No" the unkept man replied. "Sorry, you have to send one out and in some cases swim out to meet it."

So many people are waiting for their ship to come in when they've never sent one out. They anticipate receiving without first giving, reaping without sowing. They are always looking for that someone to hand them something.

A film producer friend of mine, produced a film in 2004, and has experienced the thrill of that growing movie franchise, generating over $100,000,000 from the last 5 yearly installments. To a person with a failure mindset, it looks like he was lucky, and to those who are success minded they know that it took more than luck. I've known him over ten years and consider him as someone with tremendous work ethics. Before his big break five years ago I'd seen him reading screenplay after screenplay and novel after novel looking for the right one to turn into a movie. Noticing his passionate appetite I handed him scripts that I thought would be of interest.

One day before his big break my sons and I paid him a visit. He asked if we could watch his son play in the backyard while he caught up on his script reading, I obliged. As an actor in a movie which he produced starring actor *Denzel Washington,* I saw him engrossed in a novel during the lunch break. An acquaintance of mine also told me that one day he saw him on an airplane with over six scripts in his briefcase. Today he is one of the top independent producers in Hollywood living a phenomenal lifestyle, one to be greatly desired. This is one example of a person's commitment to doing what was necessary in order to live their passion and dream. In this case, he was always reading scripts, looking for the best and right one. As you can see, he sent out many ships and they returned!

In reading this *Success 101*, you will find that in order to excel you've got to commit to growing up, and taking on the responsibilities of life. Therefore, working on one's self takes precedence.

In order to become a beautiful butterfly the caterpillar needs to first go inward and spin a cocoon. The cocoon allows it to grow and develop, focused only on these two things so it can become a beautiful butterfly. By doing so, when it emerges, it now is able to fly from flower to flower pollinating them in the process. Becoming successful is much like becoming a butterfly. It asks you to develop and focus your potential.

Each of us has talents and abilities lying dormant in us mainly because we don't have the courage to dig them up and put them to use. Many times during conversations, people who know me as an author often mention that they want to write a book or have started writing a book but have never finished it. I normally respond with, "If you really want to do it, tonight before you go to bed embark on the process of creating the outline or dust off the computer's keyboard and continue writing." How many of them do it? I can tell not many – only the ones who dare.

In his book *I Dare You* author William Danforth writes:

"I dare you to achieve something that will make the future point to you with even more pride than the present is pointing to those who have gone before you."[1]

Success is a journey. Though many think it's a destination. The people who continue to succeed value themselves and who are constantly working on changing and enhancing their self image. They feel as though they have not yet "scratched the scratch" in their chosen endeavor. They realize that success is all about taking action and dares anyone to outwork them. In essence their life has to be a worthwhile endeavor. The championship, the super bowl, the bestseller, the Oscar, the crowd's approval, the gold medal, the one million church members in attendance, and receiving of the Nobel Prize are all great accomplishments, yet those high achievers are not at all satisfied. They see the world as if it's a complex jig saw puzzle and they are the only missing piece towards the solution. They think "If it's going to be, it's up to me."

It doesn't matter who you are, where you are, where you live, what you have or don't have, who are your parents, or how low your grades are right now. You have got potential!

If you dare to make a difference, you have enlisted yourself in a great cause that will certainly bless humanity beyond your imagination. Mahatma Gandhi once said:

"Be the change you wish to see in the world."[4]

YOU no doubt by reading this book have already defined yourself as a person who wants more for their life. If you are not in pursuit of your own success, feel free to pass this volume on to someone else desiring all they have ever wanted to become. However, if you have a burning desire to go through those walls standing in your way AND if you care enough to succeed massively, AND are willing to tap into your potential - your SUCCESS is inevitable!

Is your vast potential still submerged because you need a push? Most of our potential lies dormant in us mainly because:

1. We fail to realize that we are blessed beyond measure.
2. We succumb to the effects of heartbrokenness and under appreciativeness for far too long.
3. Fear the four letter word, described as **F**alse **E**vidence **A**ppearing **R**eal; block us from becoming the best we can be.

How many times have you said **no** to your potential? How many times have you **stared** at a great opportunity in the face and said no to yourself because of your past defeats? How many times has someone told you that you can't do something or can't do all you were created to be. Most of us carry around too much junk in the trunk. The things that you and others call impossible will be yours for the taking if you eliminate that junk and choose to act.

Action is a *doing* word! Once you acquire this habit, others have no choice but to step aside for you. You are now a crusader, and the world always seems to make way for the person who knows where he or she is going.

Look at a fire engine, mission bound, speeding up your street.

I reside in Los Angeles, California and as a rule, whenever a fire engine is in pursuit – everything gives way. Despite how desperate the drivers of those now parked vehicles are, towards arriving at their destinations. Also I have witnessed dogs barking at these loaded with H_{20} passionate, purpose driven pursuing fire engines. Never once have I seen any fire engine stop to address them. Could those dogs be saying in their language "You are going too fast and making too much noise. No one can keep up, not even me. You need to slow down, don't you hear me? I am barking for you to slow down. Are you deaf?

How about those people who are content to consistently sit on their good intentions. Sitting there is one of the major causes of failure. Lackadaisically, they let opportunities pass them by. They lack the zest, the vim, the vitality as well as the ability to swim upstream, and associate with others who are content with floating downstream. They operate their lives like a train without a caboose. Then when others around them are moving ahead they become envious, wishing that these action driven individuals never succeed at their chosen vocation.

Failure to act, a fear epidemic paralyzing many would be champions in our world has a simple cure. It's action. The people who act on their ideas are not only successful, but in most cases amass great fortunes.

Some people watch things happen, some people like to wait for things happen, some people like to wonder what will happen, some people don't care what happens, but the action driven person delights in making things happen. Give a task to a busy person and they finish it speedily. Watch them go to work on it and you will notice how their actions exude confidence. He's bound to succeed.

On we learned previously, many are known to wait for their ship to come in when it has not even left the dock. "Oh, if I could just get lucky like you the go-getter" they whine. "Oh, if only I had your lucky breaks." Give your lucky breaks to them and watch them crumble. Why? Your shoes are not only uncomfortable but too big for them. They have not seen the sacrifices you have made as you keep disciplining you disappointments on a daily basis, in order to gain the stripes on your lapel or the gold medal around your neck.

What actions are you hesitant to take, knowing that by acting, your life would turn around for the better. What if the life you've always envisioned, could be heading your way, if you were to step out and meet it halfway. What actions are holding you back? Good things come to those who are filled with passion and purpose, and launch out into the deep; not to those who sit back and wait.

My mom was such a philosopher. It seems like she always knew the right thing to say. Additionally, she loved painting pictures for all nine of us, by telling stories. I recall this one she told, whenever we lagged behind upon completing our daily chores. I have used it extensively, because I feel its application. She told us about Harriet from our village who would go daily down to the river to wash clothes. Harriet would sit on this huge river stone with the soap and laundry next to her and pray that she would get help to wash the daily increasing load of clothes. Well help never came. She did not even have the courage to start. Harriet had faith, but was not willing to do the work. Consequently, help never came. About faith it is said: *Faith is the substance of things hoped for, the evidence of things not seen... Faith without works is dead.*

A few years ago I was at a business conference on the east coast and heard the keynote speaker share this story:

A very wealthy man bought a huge ranch in Arizona and invited some of his closer associates to see it. After touring the 1,500 acres of mountains, rivers, and grasslands, he took everybody to the house. The house was as spectacular as the scenery. In the back of the house was the largest swimming pool they had ever seen. However, it was filled with alligators. The owner explained:

"I value courage more than anything. It is what made me a billionaire. I value courage so much that if anyone has the courage to jump in that pool and swim to the other side, I will give them whatever they want, my land, my house, my money, anything."

Of course, everybody laughed at the challenge and turned to follow the owner into the house for lunch. Suddenly they heard a splash. Turning around they saw a guy splashing and thrashing into the water, swimming for his life as the alligators swarmed after him. After several death defying seconds, the man made it unharmed to the other side. The rich billionaire was amazed but he stuck to his promise.

He said, "You are a man of courage, you can have anything you want, house, money, land, etc., whatever you want is yours."

The swimmer, breathing heavily, looked up and said, "I just want to know who pushed me in the pool."

-*Unknown*

Some examples of being pushed into action include the story of one Alabama seamstress:

One December evening in 1955, a seamstress for a department store in Montgomery, Alabama boarded a city bus en-route to her home.

It was during the civil rights revolution, when blacks were only legally permitted to sit at the back of a bus. She walked past the "whites only" section towards the middle of the bus.

With frequent stops the bus filled up. The driver, a white man, noticed that more people of his race were still boarding. So he ordered the people in the seamstress Rosa Parks' row to move to the back of the bus. Apparently, they gave him a deaf ear. Frustrated, he barked at those black passengers. They all moved except for Rosa Parks.

Consequently, she was arrested and sent to jail after a sheriff was called to the scene.[12]

Parks' was pushed, thereby she released her potential. An act, which fueled the already simmering civil rights movement with Martin Luther King at the helm. Today in America, not only are blacks and other minorities permitted to vote but, now a black man sits in the White House as our commander and chief.

Being pushed seems to bring out the best in most people, enabling us to use more of our potential.

Less than a decade ago, I was driven to write. I never envisioned myself being a writer; frankly it was the furthest vocation from my mind.

In 1994, I attended Lee Strasburg Institute in New York and subsequently launched my acting career. I instantly fell in love with the craft. After some Off-Broadway engagements, including performances at the famous *Paper Mill Playhouse* in New Jersey, I brought my skill to Hollywood in 1996.

A few years later, several feature films as well as several national TV campaigns were under my belt. As I stated in my book, **When The Dust Settles**, I was forced into writing or to put it more subtly, it became a blessing in disguise.

While operating a modeling agency and almost going bankrupt in 2004, I stumbled into a 1970s classic film, which I so badly wanted to remake. At the time, I had no prior experience in filmmaking, except from my previous time spent on movie sets. Nonetheless, I was determined to succeed. I knew exactly how I wanted to remake this project.

For the next three weeks, I made numerous phone calls to find out who held the rights to my intended pet project. When I finally made contact with the studio, a woman answered the phone and told me they were not interested in selling the rights to a third party.

That statement didn't sit well with me. You see, in a nut shell - my plane had already taken off, the fasten-your-seat-belt signs were already extinguished, and the hostess was serving the beverage of the day. Flying was inevitable.

I composed myself, contacted a writer friend whose script was recently optioned by a major studio, and asked him to assist me in writing my script. He did one of the best things a person can do for another. Instead of giving me a fish, he showed me how to fish by sending me guidelines for writing a screenplay. I got busy writing. My mantra echoed for several months,

> "I'll write my own. I'll show them. They'll be begging for my work someday."

My imaginary airplane was swiftly gaining altitude.

I knew "if it was going to be" it was up to me! I knew where I came from and where I wanted to go. At this point I took inventory of myself and concluded that the individual who was born in St. Vincent and the Grenadines and grew up in poverty was determined to turn his world around. What I touched had to turn to gold. I Dare the ones who tried to get in my way. After my debut, writing screenplays, I experienced a supernatural divine encounter.

One day, while sitting at my desktop computer, pondering my next steps, I was led to study the life of Dr. Martin Luther King and all that he represented. He had always been my hero. I stared at his picture intermittently for several days. At that point I always desired to write my first book. I felt that I possessed very unique stories to share. So, on January 21st, 2007 after having a heart to heart, a mind over matter interlude with my hero, hidden guide, and mentor I took that leap of faith. Reflecting on what Dr. King stood for, I reasoned: If only I could do 20 % of what he stood for, I would be very happy.

So I committed my time, skill, and resources to writing consistently. In spring of 2007, my first book, **The 5 Steps to Changing Your Life** was written. With writing skills well below par, (writing as a one finger typist) I completed the first draft of that book in one week. I felt as if a dam of inspiration had flooded through my mind, as I paced back and forth from my computer to my book library. I perused through my book collection, including *The Magic of Thinking Big*, a book I read for the first time over twenty years ago. In those books I found the necessary highlighted quotes, which I needed to insert into my manuscript. While the editor worked on the book, I created the outline for my next book. It turned out to be the by-product of that inspirational deluge.

Writing my first book did not only cause me to tap into my unused potential, but brought me off the sidelines and into the game. I decided that no one was going to outwork me. Since I had never taken a typing class, I was not adept at using the computer's keyboard. My word per minute was about a few words a minute. Someone once said:

> *When the dream is big enough the facts don't count.*

In the summer of 2008, I wrote, published, and released **Spread Some Love - Relationships 101**. It's my belief that if my thoughts can produce it, it can be written.

In hindsight, I was pushed into writing. I was heaved into action towards my vocation, (a blessing in disguise) after being denied access to *that movies' rights*. The company probably meant it for evil but God meant it for good. Therefore, deciding to swim upstream was nonnegotiable. In the words of Poet Robert Frost:

> "The woods are lovely, dark and deep. But I have promises to keep, and miles to go before I sleep."[13]

Potential releasers are champions, they are action driven, stroke after stroke, play after play, day after day, even if it seems like nothing is happening. Like a duck's feet moving under water they are mentally or physically working on their game. You may not see it on the outside but it happens inside of them. The roots of a giant oak tree are submerged deep below the ground. Yes, that massive oak which withstands the wind and rain. It is as strong above the ground as it is below the ground. Its roots submerge as a result of simple mundane action in order to support that winning tree.

Yes by releasing more of your potential. You increase your value to mankind. Someone once said create a crisis daily, in other words don't wait to be pushed. Push yourself and watch what unfolds!

What do you dare to achieve using your full potential?

"IF AN ORGANIZATION DOESN'T HAVE A CLEAR PURPOSE AND SENSE OF WHAT BUSINESS IT'S IN, WE THINK THERE'S SOMETHING WRONG. YET FEW PEOPLE HAVE A CLEAR SENSE OF THEIR LIFE'S PURPOSE. HOW CAN YOU MAKE GOOD DECISIONS ABOUT HOW YOU SHOULD USE YOUR TIME IF YOU DON'T KNOW WHAT BUSINESS YOU'RE IN?"

– KEN BLANCHARD.

P 2

PURPOSE

Each of us has a purpose for our own existence. When we understand this, our life takes on new meaning. In the *The Purpose Driven Life*, Rick Warren writes:

> "Living on purpose is the only way to really live. Everything else is just existing."[2]

Too many of us drift along with the wrong crowd going nowhere fast. In *The Master Key To Riches* author Napoleon Hill recounts a statement by Andrew Carnegie, the man who developed a fortune by going the extra mile:

> *"The person who is motivated by definiteness of purpose and moves on that purpose with the spiritual forces of his being may challenge those who are indecisive at the post and pass them at*

*the grandstand. It makes no difference whether
someone is selling life insurance or digging
ditches."[3]*

It's a known fact that physically and mentally lazy
people tend to remain in their comfort zone far too
long. At that desolate place no more growth ever
occurs. Consequently, they never fully realize the good
they often might win by stepping off the sidelines and
into the game. Subsequently, their purpose remains
undefined, unsupported and un-realized. They fail
miserably in that effort to grow, stretch and become all
they can be.

We live in a world full of half-alive people who no
longer believe in themselves. Alive at age 35 but
mentally most are already dead and buried. The good
life eludes them. Any professional bodybuilder would
tell you that a muscle only grows when it's stretched.
The sleeping giants within you need to be activated.
James Allen states in *As a Man Thinketh*:

> *Those who have no central purpose in life fall an
> easy prey to petty worries, fears, troubles and
> self pitying, all of which are indications of
> weakness, which lead just as surely as
> deliberately planned sins (though by a different
> route) to failure, unhappiness, and loss. For
> weakness cannot persist in a power-evolving*

universe. We should conceive of a legitimate purpose in our hearts and set out to accomplish it. [4]

I am very intrigued by the story of this young woman. To me her account shows definiteness of purpose. Wilma Rudolph, was stricken with the polio disease at four years old. This disease usually causes people to be crippled and unable to walk. Born in poverty, her parents could not afford good medical care. To make matters worse, she was from a large family – the 20th child of 22 children. Her dad was a railroad porter and her mom a maid.

Her mom decided she would do whatever it took to help Wilma walk again. Despite the doctors saying that she would not be able to walk, her mom persisted, trying to beat the odds. She took her every week on a long bus trip to a hospital to receive therapy.

Wilma's condition didn't change, but the doctors told her mom that she needed to give Wilma a massage every day by rubbing her legs. She even taught Wilma's siblings how to do it, and they also rubbed her legs four times a day.

By the time Wilma turned 8, she could walk with a leg brace. After that, she was able to use a high topped shoe to support her foot . Wilma played basketball with her brothers every day.

One day, three years later Wilma's mom came home and found her playing basketball, not only by herself, but *bare-footed* without the aid of the special shoe.

A track coach encouraged Wilma to start running. She did, and ran so well in her senior year in high school, that she qualified for the 1956 Olympics in Melbourne, Australia. There she won a bronze medal in the women's 400-meter relay.

In 1959, she qualified for the 1960 Olympic Games in Rome, by setting a world record in the 200-meter race. At the Olympics that year, she won two gold medals: one for the 100-meter race and one for the 200-meter race.

Then accidentally, she sprained her ankle, but Wilma ignored the pain and helped her team to win **another** gold medal for the 400-meter relay! She won 3 gold medals in the Rome Olympics.

She retired from running at age 22, but went on to coach women's track teams and encourage young people.

Wilma believed that God had a greater purpose for her, so she started the Wilma Rudolph Foundation.

She passed on as a result of brain cancer in 1994, but her influence still lives on in the lives of so many young people, who look up to her leadership.[8]

There's a war to be fought. Yours! Yes, lifting your head up above the crowd will give you purpose, ammunition and direction in life. You will see where you need to go. And the world always seems to make way for the person who knows where he or she is going. Streets are crowded; a fire engine is coming through. Everything gives way; pedestrians, vehicles, everything. They all step aside for this speeding machine on a mission. Why? It has a purpose – putting out the fire and it has a sense of urgency in doing so.

THE CHAMPION

The average runner sprints
Until the breath in him is gone
But the champion has the iron will
That makes him "carry on.

For rest, the average runner begs
When limp his muscles grow
But the champion runs on leaden legs
  His spirit makes him go.

The average man's complacent

When he does his best to score
But the champion does his best
And then he does a little more.

- Author unknown.

A purpose driven individual will readily discover within that "extra-ness" necessary to overcoming all odds. The words "I can't" are totally eliminated from his or her vocabulary. Whenever he's confronted with any sign of defeat he resolves: "I am not giving up, bring it on. It might lick some, but not me. I absolutely will not be denied!" Author Julia Cameron writing in her book *The Artist's Way* says,

> "I have learned, as a rule of thumb, never to ask whether you can do something. Say, instead, that you are doing it. Then fasten your seat belt. The most remarkable thing follows."[5] Additionally she states, "Take a small step in the direction of a dream and watch the synchronous doors flying open." A maxim worth remembering, "Leap, and the net will appear."[6]

That door, one day opened for director Steven Spielberg. He visualized making a unique film. With the script already in possession he needed a producer to finance it. One day while he was walking on the beach he encountered a man who not only had the resources but was willing to invest in young film makers. This total stranger stepped up to the plate and gave Spielberg the money, enabling him to shoot *Amblin*. That film was given an honorable mention at the Venice Film Festival and opened the door for him coming to Hollywood. The rest is history.[7]

When we know what we want and embark upon accomplishing it, amazing things occur. Let's visit with some purpose driven individuals who no doubt will take away the excuses of many.

Human Activist, Helen Keller could have said "Me? I was born blind and deaf."

Inventor, Thomas A Edison could have said "Who needs an incandescent light bulb? I have already tried 10,999 times."

Steve Jobs, the founder of Apple computers, could have said "I'm way too young to achieve massive success." He made his first million at age twenty-three, his first ten million at twenty-four, and at age twenty-five his first 100 million.

President Abraham Lincoln could have said "I am a big failure politically. I have already lost eighteen elections. I would never become the American president."

President, Nelson Mandela could have said "My own country men threw me in jail, where I've spent most of my life. I could never become the president of my country."

Colonel Sanders, the founder of Kentucky Fried Chicken could have said "I dropped out of high school plus I 'm way over 40 - way too old to succeed in life." He didn't fulfill his dream until age 65 and received 1,009 "NO'S" before he got a "YES."[8]

Paul Getty, the world's first billionaire could have said "I'm not born a businessman. I have no business being in business." Yet he became a model for some of the most successful business people of our time. Getty said,

> "I'd rather have 1 % of the efforts of a hundred men than 100% of my own efforts."[9]

He owns the Getty Museum in Los Angeles, California. One of my associates, about this huge landmark remarks: "Getty owns a mountain and that's the only man I know to do so."

President, John F. Kennedy could have said "I am too young to become the American president; no one is going to listen to me."

President, Truman could have said "I have never been

to college I could never become president of America."

Artists, Ray Charles and Stevie Wonder could have said "We are blind, how are we going to find the keys to the piano, much less sing to an audience who we cannot see."

Charlie Chaplin, one of history's wealthiest actors could have said "I grew up in poverty roaming the streets of London. I'll never amass a fortune."

Astronaut, Neil Armstrong could have said 'The moon is so out of reach, I have no business going up there."

Most people lack the initiative needed in order to become all they were meant to be, mainly because they don't believe deep down inside that they are valuable. Therefore they live a purpose deprived life.

Purpose, a *directive* word, which means heading towards something, gains momentum when meshed with the *propellant* word belief – that feeling knowing that you can do whatever you set out to do. People, lacking the propellant in their own mindset and philosophy usually look for this additive coming from someone else's, and when they don't receive it, they wonder why their life spins around like a top in mud – going nowhere fast. In order to take advantage of

others believing in you, you must first harness
the power of belief in yourself.

When a commercial airplane is getting ready for
takeoff, first the doors are closed shut. Passenger's seat
belts are securely fastened. The plane then taxis down
the runway in preparation for takeoff. The air traffic
controllers in the control tower are aware that the
plane is ready for takeoff. Instruction is then given to
the pilot to speed up. He releases the throttle, retracts
the landing gear and engages the skies.

Believing in yourself will initiate purpose. Belief: that
ability necessary to taxi down the runway in your
preparation for takeoff.   As soon as others start
believing in you, your ascent becomes eminent. *All
things are possible to him who believes.* Successful
people believed that they were going to be successful
and set sail in pursuit of their objective. Their lives
became driven by that burning desire to succeed. They
knew where they were going and consequently found
their hidden guides to take them there. It is often said

"When   the   student   is   ready   the   teacher
appears."

As an immigrant to the United States several years
ago, I sensed that Americans are so fortunate because
of the many opportunities which exist in this country,

and that they often take their heritage for granted.

Conversely, back then I felt like the odds were stacked against me, coming from the Caribbean and not being able to master the Standard American English. I still speak with an island flavor. Nevertheless, I learned to grasp those opportunities which could lead me to the next level.

Consequently, some amazing people have stepped into my life as guides, including my mentor and friend Bob Wilson. He had just retired after teaching elementary and high school teacher for a period of 35 years. We first met when he played my Dad in a student film - the adaptation of *Guess Who Is Coming To Dinner*. This was my first film project when I moved to Hollywood in 1996. He has always guided me back on the right path, especially during those early years of my divorce, and has played the role of a devil's advocate on numerous occasions. Addition-ally, Bob has helped me to validate my belief in myself, as I dare to make a difference.

Belief in self is paramount if there is ever going to be any worthwhile accomplishment. Remember, no one else really believes in you until you first believe in yourself.

If an organization doesn't have a clear

purpose and sense of what business it's in, we think there's something wrong. Yet few people have a clear sense of their life's purpose. How can you make good decisions about how you should use your time if you don't know what business you're in? Ken Blanchard, *Leading At A Higher Level.*

Once you are airborne, and the fasten-your-seatbelt sign is off, you are now not only committed to fly to your destination with a purpose in mind, but at what speed.

What do you think is your purpose in life.

"DEVELOP A PASSION FOR LEARNING. IF YOU DO, YOU WILL NEVER CEASE TO GROW."

-ANTHONY J. D'ANGELO

P 3

PASSION

You have already tapped into your potential, you understand your purpose, but how driven are you towards becoming the person you were really meant to be? Some people live their lives in a lukewarm "whatever happens" state. Water is known to boil at 211 degrees and at 212 degrees turn to steam enough to push any locomotive. That extra one degree has propelled many from failure to amazing success.

Do you have the zeal to make things happen? When you feel that zest, excitement, focus and a burning desire to accomplish something: that's passion running through your being. Without your passion, no one will see your potential. There's plenty of room at the top but not too many are passionate enough about getting there. That's why they never arrive. They act as if they have forever to live and unfortunately the successful-good-life eludes them.

Everything that exists was first an idea acted upon either by you or someone else. As a writer I've met so many people with an idea for the next bestseller or the next hit movie and yet they never write it.

Consequently their idea never makes it to the book shelf or the screen. What would happen if you were told that you only have ONE month to live? How zealous would you be about getting things done? Would that back burner where "dreams that can wait" are stored be full or empty? What would be your commitment level, 10, 90 or 150?

Some people like to watch things happen, some people like to wonder what will happen, and some people don't really care what happens. But the action-driven person delights in making things happen. Become branded for doing things. When you see something that ought to be done, step up to the plate and hit the home run. Once you acquire the action habit, others have no choice but to step aside for you. Take one step forward in the direction of your goals and dreams and your adversaries will run for cover. They see your obvious passion and determination.

In *The 5 Steps To Changing Your Life* I also related a story about a young man who was working as a second hand on a railroad. His thoroughness subsequently won him an opportunity to work in a shipping office. During the interim the substitute clerk asked this young man for some facts and figures. The young man didn't know anything about bookkeeping, but he spent three days and three nights without sleep and had the facts ready for the superintendent when he returned. That passionate act of decision and commitment later propelled him into the vice-presidency seat of his own company.

Successful people make it a habit of getting things done while unsuccessful people are habitual procrastinators. A successful person sees a great opportunity such as to go into business for himself while the unsuccessful person doesn't take action and that trend passes him by. He subsequently misses out on the opportunity to become a profiteer and resorts himself to the status of a consumer.

The great opportunities in life are captured by those who take action, not by those who wait. "The early bird catches the worm" while the late bird removes the dirt in hope of finding worms.
Let's visit with a passionate driven individual, Bill Gates, who did what it took to make his goals and

dreams come true. Notice he didn't let things get in the way.

In 1975 Bill Gates dropped out of Harvard to pursue his career as a software designer. He later was joined by his colleague Paul Allen in the co-founding venture of Microsoft. It was rumored that Gates also showed the concept to two of his other colleagues who said no. Other sources claimed that Gates had a cot in his office that he slept on night after night for several years when he was getting Microsoft off the ground. In 1980 Gates developed the Microsoft Disk Operating System (MS-DOS). And he successfully sold IBM on this new operating system.

By the 1990s Microsoft had sold more than 100 million copies of MS-DOS making the operating system the all-time leader in software sales.

Gates' competitive drive and fierce desire to win has made him a powerful force in business. It was his passion for his product and what it would do for the world that kept him committed to endure setbacks, such as lawsuits he encountered along the way. It also consumed much of his personal life. In the six years between 1978 and 1984, he took a total of only two weeks vacation. On New Year's Day 1994 Gates married Melinda French, a Microsoft manager, on the Hawaiian island of Lanai. His fortune at the time of his marriage was estimated at close to seven billion dollars. By 1997 his worth was estimated at approximately $37 billion, earning him the title of "Richest man in America."

His contributions really amaze me.

Aside from being the most famous businessman of the late 1990s, Gates also has distinguished himself as a philanthropist. He and wife Melinda established the Bill & Melinda Gates Foundation, which focuses on helping to improve health care and education for children around the world. The foundation has donated $4 billion since its start in 1996. Recent pledges include $1 billion over twenty years to fund college scholarships for about one thousand minority students; $750 million over five years to help launch the Global Fund for Children's Vaccines; $50 million to help the World Health Organization's efforts to eradicate polio, a crippling disease that usually attacks children; and $3 million to help prevent the spread of acquired immune deficiency syndrome (AIDS; an incurable disease that destroys the body's immune system) among young people in South Africa. In November 1998 Gates and his wife also gave the largest single gift to a U.S. public library, when they donated $20 million to the Seattle Public Library.

Another of Gates' charitable donations was $20 million given to the Massachusetts Institute of Technology to build a new home for its Laboratory for Computer Science.

In July 2000 the foundation gave John Hopkins University a five-year, $20 million grant to study whether or not inexpensive vitamin and mineral pills can help save lives in poor countries. On November 13, 2000, Harvard University's School of Public Health announced it had received $25 million from the foundation to study AIDS prevention in Nigeria. The grant was the largest single private grant in the school's history. It was announced on February 1, 2001, that the foundation would donate $20 million to speed up the global eradication (to completely erase) of the disease commonly known as elephantiasis, a disease that causes disfigurement. In 2002 Gates, along with rock singer Bono, announced plans for DATA Agenda, a $24 billion fund (partially supported by the Bill and Melinda Gates Foundation) that seeks to improve health care in Africa.[3]

Although Gates' parents had a law career in mind for their son, he developed his early interest for computers which turned into his passion, resulting in the Microsoft phenomenon. Additionally, Gates attributes his success to reading the biographies of successful people over a long period of time. His philanthropic life-style and contribution to technology continues to make a passionate difference.

In your quest to succeed, there are three questions which you can always ask yourself. How high and how far do I want to go? Who do I want to take with me? and When do I want to begin?

These next two brothers understood the benefits of asking and answering those three questions. The wanted to fly:

Orville and Wilbur Wright grew up in the 1800s - 1900s. These brothers wanted to construct an airplane that flew. People viewed them as doubly insane. No one had ever accomplished such a feat. "That's highly impossible," they reasoned. In bars, restaurants, buses, even churches – everywhere people gathered, this became a topic of discussion. In addition, while Orville and Wilbur worked on their invention, scientific studies were carried out to prove that a body heavier than air could not possibly fly.

Here's more on their journey:

In 1899, after Wilbur Wright had written a letter of request to the Smithsonian Institution for information about flight experiments, the Wright Brothers designed their first aircraft: a small, biplane glider flown as a kite to test their solution for controlling the craft by wing warping. Wing warping is a method of arching the wingtips slightly to control the aircraft's rolling motion and balance.

The Wrights spent a great deal of time observing birds in flight. They noticed that birds soared into the wind and that the air flowing over the curved surface of their wings created lift. Birds change the shape of their wings to turn and maneuver. They believed that they could use this technique to obtain roll control by warping, or changing the shape, of a portion of the wing.

Over the next three years, Wilbur and his brother Orville would design a series of gliders which would be flown in both unmanned (as kites) and piloted flights. They read about the works of Cayley, and Langley, and the hang-gliding flights of Otto Lilienthal. They corresponded with Octave Chanute concerning some of their ideas. They recognized that control of the flying aircraft would be the most crucial and hardest problem to solve.

Following a successful glider test, the Wrights built and tested a full-size glider. They selected Kitty Hawk, North Carolina as their test site because of its wind, sand, hilly terrain and remote location.

In 1900, the Wrights successfully tested their new 50-pound biplane glider with its 17-foot wingspan and wing-warping mechanism at Kitty Hawk, in both unmanned and piloted flights. In fact, it was the first piloted glider. Based upon the results, the Wright Brothers planned to refine the controls and landing gear, and build a bigger glider.

In 1901, at Kill Devil Hills, North Carolina, the Wright Brothers flew the largest glider ever flown, with a 22-foot wingspan, a weight of nearly 100 pounds and skids for landing. However, many problems occurred: the wings did not have enough lifting power; forward elevator was not effective in controlling the pitch; and the wing-warping mechanism occasionally caused the airplane to spin out of control. In their disappointment, they predicted that man will probably not fly in their lifetime.

In spite of the problems with their last attempts at flight, the Wrights reviewed their test results and determined that the calculations they had used were not reliable. They decided to build a wind tunnel to test a variety of wing shapes and *their effect on lift. Based upon these tests, the inventors had a greater understanding of how an airfoil (wing) works and could calculate with greater accuracy how well a particular wing design would fly. They planned to design a new glider with a 32-foot wingspan and a tail to help stabilize it.*

During 1902, the brothers flew numerous test glides using their new glider. Their studies showed that a movable tail would help balance the craft and the Wright Brothers connected a movable tail to the wing-warping wires to coordinate turns. With successful glides to verify their wind tunnel tests, the inventors planned to build a powered aircraft.

After months of studying how propellers work the Wright Brothers designed a motor and a new aircraft sturdy enough to accommodate the motor's weight and vibrations. The craft weighed 700 pounds and came to be known as the Flyer.

The brothers built a movable track to help launch the Flyer. This downhill track would help the aircraft gain enough airspeed to fly. After two attempts to fly this machine, one of which resulted in a minor crash, Orville Wright took the Flyer for a 12-second, sustained flight on

December 17, 1903. This was the first successful, powered, piloted flight in history.

In 1904, the first flight lasting more than five minutes took place on November 9. The Flyer II was flown by Wilbur Wright.

In 1908, passenger flight took a turn for the worse when the first fatal air crash occurred on September 17. Orville Wright was piloting the plane. Orville Wright survived the crash, but his passenger, Signal Corps Lieutenant Thomas Selfridge, did not. The Wright Brothers had been allowing passengers to fly with them since May 14, 1908.

In 1909, the U.S. Government bought its first airplane, a Wright Brothers biplane, on July 30. The airplane sold for $25,000 plus a bonus of $5,000 because it exceeded 40 mph.

In 1911, the Wrights' Vin Fiz was the first airplane to cross the United States. The flight took 84 days, stopping 70 times. It crash-landed so many times that little of its original building materials were still on the plane when it arrived in California. The Vin Fiz was named after a grape soda made by the Armour Packing Company.[23]

As a result of their passion to fly, we can now travel in an airplane from New York to London, Paris, Rome and other cross continental cities in less than six hours. Many of us are afraid to launch out passionately, mainly, because we are so afraid of failing.

If you want to become a champion, I believe that it is a good thing to jump off with your ideas, and see who would catch you. You just never know!

Which situation could you change for the better if you are passionate about making a difference in the world?

"WHEN PEOPLE FEEL GOOD ABOUT YOU AND THEMSELVES DURING THE TIMES THEY'RE WITH YOU, THEN YOUR LEVEL OF INFLUENCE INCREASES SIGNIFICANTLY."

- JOHN MAXWELL

P 4

PERSONALITY

Successful people always seem to exude that indescribable quality which attracts you to them like freckles of steel to magnet. You feel it in their handshake, their pat on the back. You hear it in their intonations, their looking you in the eye, and in their charismatic smile. They totally have "IT" and it's called personality. They draw you in. Indescribable, yet it moves you.

➢ Where does personality come from?
➢ Is it something we are born with?
➢ Can it be developed?
➢ How do we get it?

It can be acquired if you are willing to work on yourself.

Benjamin Franklin began as a printer's apprentice and later became the first self made millionaire in America. He adapted a process of personal development strategies. As a young man he struggled realizing that he was somewhat ill mannered and argumentative, character traits which he realized was creating animosity toward him from his co-workers and associates as well. In an effort to change he rewrote the script of his personality. Franklin began by making a list of what that ideal person should possess.

Franklin then concentrated on developing one virtue each week. Some of those thirteen virtues included: tranquility, moderation, resolution, humility, order and temperance. He practiced and worked hard at these virtues. As a routine he would practice one virtue each week, then two weeks, then three weeks, then for a one month period until it became a part of his character.

As a result he not only became one of the most popular personalities but also very influential as well. His influence played a very important role as an ambassador from the United States during the constitutional convention, when the constitution and the Bill of Rights for the United States was debated, negotiated and agreed upon.[2] By daring to work on himself he made himself into a person capable of shaping the course of history.

Some people have a greater capacity for developing personality traits more than others. And this has a lot to do with their social upbringing. A child who is raised in a home where there is "high and high standards," is more likely to develop these personality traits. However, many others overcome adversity and chose to develop these personality traits moving in the direction of success.

The people who've learned from their failures like Benjamin Franklin have been knocked down so many times that they not only embrace "getting back up" with a smile but embraced the adversity simultaneously, knowing that they will get back up and you better watch out when they do. Successful people tend to turn "IT" on like magic. Their magnetism wins you and draws you in wanting to know more about them.

I've always made it a habit to learn something from the personality of every successful person I've encountered. Most of all I've noticed and admired this special trait, which is a characteristic of great leadership - the ability to solve problems. Obstacles have no chance, at least not for long. They have that leaders' mindset.

When I first met Mr. Stonecipher he greeted me with a firm handshake, and he conveyed in his "good to meet you" the message that "John the world needs you."

That interaction spoke directly to my potential. That exchange gave such a tremendous boast to my self-esteem. How can I ever forget about my destiny whenever I associate with personalities like him?

Have you ever seen someone enter a room and immediately – charismatically – attract the warmth and attention of others? Understand, they were not born this way. One thing is for sure, they have become this way as a result of their many trials and failures as well as successes along the way. They have learned how to laugh at the adversities life brings their way. Personalities who have made success their vocation are like that whether you meet them on the top of a mountain or down in a valley. In good times or bad, they have the knack for attracting people.

These twelve traits speak volume about an individual with an attractive personality.

1. He has conquered selfishness, others have become his priority.
2. He knows that he'll reap what he sows. Therefore he sows his best.
3. He exercises self control.
4. He listens to others.
5. He gives with no strings attached.
6. He recognizes value in others.
7. He appreciates what others intend, not only what they do.

8. He lifts others up.
9. He's positive about life.
10. He leads and inspires others. When people leave his presence they feel better about themselves.
11. He is a servant leader.
12. He keeps increasing his own value.

His leadership has influence. He lifts you to higher ground. Brian Tracy, in his book *Million Dollar Habits* writes:

> Make it a habit to go through life doing and saying the things that raise the self-esteem of others and make them feel valuable.[3]

In his book *Becoming a Person of Influence* John Maxwell writes:

> When people feel good about you and themselves during the times they're with you, then your level of influence increases significantly.[1]

By now I hope you have a new outlook on life with a new feeling about yourself. By adopting the personality traits outlined in this chapter, you would discover it is easiest for you to meet the needs of others once your needs has been met. You would become a people magnet attracting others who will support you getting towards the next level and your destiny. Consequently, a domino effect is created causing others to win because you've won.

How do you measure up to the 12 traits?

"You will never make it upstream with only a mere wish. The rapids are fierce; they'll push you back downstream toward self pity and mediocrity if your resolve isn't strong enough."

-John A. Andrews

"NOTHING IN THE WORLD CAN TAKE THE PLACE OF PERSISTENCE. TALENT WILL NOT. NOTHING IN THE WORLD IS MORE COMMON THAN UNSUCCESSFUL PEOPLE WITH TALENT. GENIUS WILL NOT. UNREWARDED GENIUS IS ALMOST A PROVERB. EDUCATION WILL NOT. THE WORLD IS FULL OF EDUCATED DERELICTS. PERSISTENCE, DETERMINATION AND HARD WORK MAKE THE DIFFERENCE."

— CALVIN COOLIDGE

P 5

PERSISTENCE

We've now come to one of the most important chapters in this book. This embodies the defining quality between people who succeed and the ones who don't. You know yourself and the potential inside, you have a purpose, you have developed passion, acquired a magnetic personality, created a vision for your life and found the right time to launch it. You leave no road for retreat. In other words "you burn the ships" the bridge gets demolished. There's no way out. You are persistent. Therefore, success becomes inevitable.

In *Think and Grow Rich*, Napoleon Hill recounts this story:

> A great warrior was faced with a situation which made it necessary for him to make a decision

which ensured him success on the battlefield. This leader was about to send his armies against a powerful foe, whose men fearfully outnumbered his. He got busy and loaded his soldiers in boats, sailed to the enemy's country, unloaded soldiers and equipment. Then he gave the orders to burn the ships that had carried them. Addressing his men before the first battle, he said "You see the boats going up in smoke. That means that we cannot leave these shores alive unless we win! We now have no choice-we *win*-or *we perish!*" They won.[2]

All successful people have in common this particular trait. They have learned how to develop the habit of persistency towards setting and reaching their goals. Their "not giving up mindset and philosophy" separates them from the rest of the world. They know that without determination they will never arrive at their destination. So they persist in spite of the obstacles which are presented along the way. They become masters of the art of getting back up when they get knocked down.

In order to succeed in today's world and make a difference one needs to not only learn from their successes but also from their failures. One ought to be able to look back at those diametrically opposed experiences and say "This is what I did in order to succeed and this is what I've learned. This is what I did that caused me to fail and this is what I've learned. "

Persistence has so much to do with strong faith. Faith is described as "the evidence of things not seen." Persistence calls for a strong, unwavering faith, one capable of moving mountains along the way.

I moved to Hollywood, California in July 1996 as an actor. Within those first two years I landed nine TV commercials in a thirteen month span. I then experienced a journey dominated by failures. So much that, constantly being beaten up by life in Hollywood led me to believe that every seed that I planted was killed by haters and player haters alike. Those industry pythons who made it their duty to destroy the kernels before they grew up much less bear fruit. They delighted in squeezing my dreams out of me. Never! They had it coming. I decided that I was going to start believing in myself.

I knew where I came from and where I wanted to go. The boy from the islands of Saint Vincent and the Grenadines, who, went to school at times without shoes on his feet? I had had enough and was going from here on to make a significant difference. What I touched had to turn to gold. Dare the ones who tried to stop me or get in the way. I was like a rhino coming through. Failure wasn't going to be an alternative. I was going through whatever stood in my way, en-route to my destiny.

While I had written several screenplays, I had always wanted to etch my first book. I felt that I had very unique stories to share. So, on January 21st, 2007 after having a heart to heart, a mind over matter interlude with my hidden guide and mentor the late Dr. Martin Luther King Jr., I took that tremendous leap of faith. As I looked at his picture several times, reflecting on what he stood for, if only I could do 20 % of what he stood for I'd be very happy. Releasing just one percent of my untapped potential could make a significant difference in the world. So I launched out and wrote my first book, *The 5 Steps To Changing Your Life*. Believing that I had what it took to write it.

While pondering my own legacy, I knew that I had not done enough for mankind and myself. I stared at MLK's quote:

> *"Take the first step in faith, you don't have to see the whole staircase. Just take the first step."*[3]

For well over 30 minutes, consumed by it and all that he stood for, I passionately outlined my first book *The 5 Steps to Changing Your Life*.

My contribution towards changing mindsets at this point took center stage. If I could help to change the mindset and philosophy of one dream deprived individual, this world would become a better place I reasoned.

So, through inspiration I was moved to write my first book. That night I opened up my writing software, outlined the first draft and begun writing my first book. I felt as if a dam of inspiration was released from my mind. I kept going back and forth to my book library looking for quotes to supplement my written thoughts. There, I was able to retrieve books which I had previously read. I scanned through their pages, locating the exact high-lighted quote necessary for insert into my waiting text. I felt possessed with - the Michael Jordan like feeling when he dumped 69 points on the Cleveland Cavaliers. Inspiration took over and I passionately completed the first draft of that volume in one week.

An editor and cover designer stepped up to the plate as if summoned by some unknown guide. I must admit that I spoke with several designers over a 3 month span who'd promised to work with me on the project but never did. Finally the right one showed up. He found exactly the image I was looking for and the book was published in June of 2007. My book was released and made available on Amazon and at other online stores. I was ecstatic!

One of my clients at that time, a well known celebrity who I chauffeured, learned about my new book and promised to give me a "blurb" after reading it. The book was delivered as requested. I waited for the blurb and have never heard back from her since. Nevertheless, my book received endorsements from other sources. Meanwhile my boss, who was her good friend, pulled the cord on me - I was out of a job. He'd heard my sirens coming and knew that my mindset and philosophy was not that of a settler.

These turn of events wasn't because of a failed marriage but someone who couldn't see success for himself. Therefore, he didn't want it for me. In addition my roommate at the time said he didn't need the money but I had taken so many of his excuses away during our dwelling together. He couldn't stand my velocity; he knew that with my tenacity I'd out-work anybody. While he slept I wrote. Consequently, after weeks of unemployment I once again found myself homeless. A situation I detested and was unprepared for. YET I WAS NOT GOING TO BE DENIED! I WAS DETERMINED TO BECOME AN AUTHOR REGARDLESS OF MY CIRCUMSTANCES.

Back in 2007, while my editor edited my first book, I started writing *Keep Love Alive*. I later titled the volume *Spread Some Love (Relationships 101)* in order to cover the basics on relationships. Martin Luther King day the next year (2008) rolled around and I was once again haunted by my lack of accomplishments in life thus far. In spite of my recurring adversity, on MLK day of 2008 I printed out the first completed draft of my new book. With all the time management skills I'd gleaned through the years, without inspiration, I don't know if I could have pulled that off. Inspiration led me to action once again and I created my own break instead of sitting around looking for it. I felt like I was born to write.

In early April 2008 I founded my own publishing company, Books That Will Enhance Your Life. I published the Amazon kindle edition of the book. A few weeks later the e-book and paperback versions were published and released thereafter.

Upon receiving the proof of *Spread Some Love - Relationships 101*. I kissed it several times. A friend was with me at the time and jokingly said, "You kissed yourself" For those of you who have seen the book you will notice that I've used one of my headshots on the front cover. To him I replied "Yes." If only he knew how much value I saw in this product. I knew that I had brought something of significance to the world.

A bookstore chain refused from stocking my book on their shelves. They flat out said "We are not going to carry that title because the author published it through a small independent publisher." and additionally "it didn't fit our model." That ticked me off because (a) I founded and owned that publishing company *Books That Will Enhance Your Life* and (b) I wrote the book in addition to owning the rights to it. That didn't sit too well with me, so I went undercover.

Their booksellers claimed that it was not modeled for their store. Well, based on my research, I found out that if a store really wanted to carry a book as long as it was available from one of the major distributors and was returnable, they could shortlist that book. But instead they were saying flat out that they were not going to carry the title, "why?" I pried further.

By this time I had refused from taking their "No" for an answer. In less than three weeks after doing my research and going on a tirade with them, they stocked my book in several of their California bookstores. That led to more stores following suite on the East Coast. When someone said no I purposefully pushed for the YES and got it.

Through Word Of Mouth marketing my book had already arrived on shelves not only in California but also on the East coast as well. So much that the constant flow of orders from that particular title alerted their corporate office according to their spokesperson. My sub publisher contacted me to make sure there had not been any fraud involved.

As far as I knew people were just flat out ordering copies of the book. My phone line was burning up with inquiries about this new title. Friends were telling other friends about it just like a good movie. WOM marketing had the advantage. The small press acquisition department for that book chain dragged their feet with my title submission for national distribution. In the meantime I had already secured my first major book-signing event with one of their local stores.

The upcoming signing was creating such a buzz, so much that a major entertainment TV station proposed to cover me along with the event. However, they pulled out one day before the event. They claimed that they weren't able to get a host interviewer to cover for that weekend. I immediately got on the phone and organized my own camera crew. Even a freelance stylist provided her services on my behalf.

The day arrived. I showed up excited and dressed to the nines, after all it was my first major book signing event. All eyes were on me. The very inspirational on-camera interview ended, and then it was on to the book signing event. In less than a few hours all the books they had in stock were sold out much to the surprise of their management team. Their cash registers were going Cha Ching – Cha Ching - Cha Ching. I watched as "Spread Some Love Relationships 101" exited in shopping bags.

Those results still did not influence the small press into a nationwide - in - store placement of the volume. They came up with every worn out excuse under the sun including me possibly trying a later resubmission of the title. I later learned that if they don't want to bring you in they will find every excuse in the book.

While they were dealing with indecision at that department surrounding acquisition of my book, the visionary in me operated at full throttle. I was busy creating the script for a docu-drama based on the book. The book had already sold thousands of copies without any publicity within the first four months. It was already apparent to me that people were hungry relationally. Therefore, no matter how long the current recession lasted, I knew that relationship minded individuals were still going to be working on their relationships. I continued to move forward with my writing, and in addition produced my docu-drama based on relationships.

In the spring of 2010, after publishing my fifteenth book, I decided to turn my screenplay Rude Buay ... the Unstoppable into a novel. This script, an action thriller set in Jamaica, Miami, and Columbia was written seven years ago and introduced to few major production houses in Hollywood. They saw the potential and gave it thumbs up. Yet, no one was willing to put their money where their mouth was. In the summer of that same year I published and released Rude Buay ... The Unstoppable. Knowing that I had a great project, I planned and embarked on a cross country tour of over 35 states and almost 100 cities. The title is now a national bestseller, and today I just landed in New York City after a two week tour signing for the two major book chains in Puerto Rico, Hawaii, Southern and Northern California. Puerto Rico and Hawaii are two of the locations selected to shoot this upcoming film.

IT COULDN'T BE DONE

Somebody said it couldn't be done,
But he with a chuckle replied
That "maybe it couldn't," but he would be one
Who wouldn't say till he'd tried,

So he buckled right in with the trace of a grin
On his face. If he worried, he'd hid it.
Somebody scoffed: "Oh, you'll never do that;

At least no one ever has done it.
But he took off his coat and he took off his hat,

And the first thing we know he begun it.
With a lift of his chin and a bit of a grin,
Without any doubting or "quiddit"
He started to sing as he tackled the thing

That couldn't be done, and he did it.
There are thousands to tell you it cannot be done,
There are thousands to prophesy failure;
There are thousands to point out to you one by one;

The dangers that wait to assail you.
But just buckle in with a bit of a grin,
Just take off your coat and go to it
Just start in to sing as you tackle the thing
That "cannot be done" and you'll do it.

--Unknown

You will find that most successful people have all encountered failure along their path to success. Some, many times, others hundreds of times, while some ranked as high as in thousands of times – as in the case of Thomas A. Edison. The most important element in their accomplishment is that they never gave up.

Once again another example of persistence - determination to succeed.

Any successful person will tell you that it takes focus, strong character and determination in order to succeed. This applies to all areas of their lives. Several years ago after my divorce, I got immersed into the subject of relationships and have written several books on the subject since. I've noticed that many people work hard on their jobs and not on their relationships. As a result they end up in divorce and wonder why their marriage hasn't worked. They missed the embodiment of this chapter you are now reading. Persistence starts with knowing that you have what it takes to succeed.

Are you ready for the climb amidst the turbulence in order to acquire success?

How is your thought process?

This is one of my favorite poems because it sums up my philosophy on determination.

If you think you are beaten, you are,
If you think you dare not, you don't.
If you like to win, but you think you can't,
It is almost certain you won't.

If you think you'll lose, you are lost,
For out in this world we find,
Success begins with a fellow's will-
It's all in the state of mind.

If you think you are outclassed, you are,
You've got to think high to rise,
You've got to be sure of yourself before
You can ever win a prize.

Life's battles don't always go
To the stronger or faster man,
But soon or late the man who wins
Is the man WHO THINKS HE CAN!

-    Unknown

Most people never get to experience the other 90% of their potential. They never experience the thrill of sweet success. They fear getting knocked down. Nobody has ever accomplished anything worthwhile without being tested and tried. Successful people are winners; they let nothing stand in their way of victory. You can smell their tenacity like expensive cologne because they have a feeling of their own worth. They think: I can. I will and I shall not be denied.

The power of your purpose depends on the vigor and determination behind it. And your determination is

necessary to take that ball into the end zone and score that winning touchdown.

First you have to believe though, really believe that you can become successful before you do. "We do not attract that which we want but that which we are."5 It has to be a mindset. And success is a process which takes patience. We live in a microwave age where everything is instant. Instant this and instant that. Well, there is no such thing as instant success. Success is never like the Jack and the Beanstalk scenario. It is never a fairy tale but the complete opposite. It is a Farming 101 mindset – sowing and reaping.

Sometimes other people don't see what we do while we are in the trenches in order to acquire our success. Most times they only see the end result and mistakenly call it luck.

I am always reminded of how a Chinese bamboo tree whenever I think about determination. Success calls for great determination. Ask any successful person.

> *You take a little seed and plant, water, and fertilize it for a whole year, and nothing happens.*

> *The second year you water and fertilize it, and nothing happens.*

The third year you water and fertilize it, and nothing yet.

The fourth year you water and fertilize it, and still nothing.

The fifth year you continue to water and fertilize the seed. Sometime during the fifth year, the Chinese bamboo tree sprouts and grows NINETY FEET IN SIX WEEKS.

Most often success is like that Chinese bamboo tree, requiring you to hang in there much longer before seeing the fruits of your labor. Many misunderstand the process and view success like throwing on a superman outfit – such a temporary ordeal. Don't be mistaken, it goes much deeper than that. No wonder it becomes unnervingly uncomfortable for most failures to be in the presence of the successful for too long because that successful person quickly takes their excuses away.

According to Malcolm Gladwell in his book *Outliers*

"What is the question we always ask about the successful? We want to know what they're like – what kind of personalities they have, or how intelligent they are, or what kind of lifestyles they have, or what special talents they might have

been born with. And we assume that it is those personal qualities that explain how that individual reached the top."[6] He continues: "In the autobiographies published every year by the billionaire/entrepreneur/rock star/celebrity, the story line is always the same: our hero is born in modest circumstances and by virtue of his own grit and talent fights his way to greatness."[7]

Let me introduce you to an athlete whose persistence produced brilliance.

Michael Phelps made it a habit of working out in the pool for 8 hours a day for several years in order to accomplish Olympic excellence.

Michael Phelps, winner of several gold medals during the 2009 Olympics made it a habit of working out in the pool for 8 hours a day for several years in order to accomplish Olympic distinction. It was said that "One component of Michael Phelps' phenomenal success is his "made-for-swimming" physique. But the main component is the carefully-crafted training program that his coach, Bob Bowman, has created for him." Let's pick up on his journey to Olympic excellence as described by Bowman:

Here, Coach Bowman-the 2001 ASCA Coach of the Year-describes his training protocols and provides sample workouts.

I think it was pretty clear from the beginning that Michael Phelps was a special swimmer. When he joined us at North Baltimore Aquatic Club as a 7-year-old, he was a baseball/ soccer/ lacrosse athlete.

His first year, he just did a 60minute, once-a-week stroke clinic with our aquatics director, Cathy Lears. His training and intensity escalated from there to where, by the time he was 10 and setting NAG records, he was better than many of the older swimmers.

Obviously, we had to do some rapid lane promotions.

To those who knew the Phelps aquatic heritage, his prowess was no surprise. His oldest sister, Hilary, was a national-level swimmer. His second sister, Whitney, was also a 200 flyer. She made the 1994 World Championship team that competed in Rome, and she still holds the 11 - 12 NAG record in the 100 yard fly.

So, in many ways, swimming excellence has been a family trait. And while it is also tempting to think of Michael only in terms of the fly and

IM, a review of his record reveals a litany of national rankings in the free and back as well.

Supportive parents have aided his climb immensely. They had been through the drill with the older daughters.

Then there's Michael's physique: at 6-4, he is mostly torso with a large chest and long arms. It's a body great for swimming. He is very flexible throughout the shoulders, upper body and especially in the ankles.

Michael is much more disciplined than he was in his earlier days. He was, and is still, a pretty strong-willed kid. Back then, he didn't understand he might have to do some things he didn't want to do, like train, sit still, pay attention and not talk. He was very energetic as a young boy.

These days, he's modified his behavior-either voluntarily or involuntarily. I think part of that modification started when I pulled him out of the pool and told him, "You've got a stroke that is going to set a world record some day, and you are going to do it in practice."

Michael has an athletic mentality second to

none. He is keenly competitive, and that's what drives him. In competition, he is incredibly focused and able to relax. The higher the level of competition, the better he is. That's something you just don't see very often.

What he needs to work on is the same thing he had to work on as a child: to strengthen the connection in his mind between what happens on a daily basis and how that affects what's going to happen when he gets in the big meet. He's better now and better than 90 percent of the population, but he still has those days-about once every six weeks-when he's tired, and it's a struggle for me to get him to do things and maintain the same intensity in workout that he gives in the big meets.

In 2002, he had an excellent summer, setting a world record in the 400 meter IM, taking four events at the Phillips 66 Summer Nationals, notching American records in the 200 IM and 100 fly and swimming the fastest fly leg ever in a 4 x 100 world record medley relay victory.

In addition to water work, we religiously incorporated a "Mike Barrowman medicine ball routine" into his dryland routine, and we did a threeweek stay at altitude in Colorado Springs.

He's followed his long course success with the best fall and winter he's ever had-by far.

Typically, for the last three or four years, Michael has had very good summers. Then there have been down periods in the fall where we've had to work hard to crank him back up to a good mental mode. That has not been the case this year.

This fall and winter, Michael has worked hard on the backstroke. In fact, he's gotten really good. Recently, he finished a 15 x 200 yard back set with a 1:45. Not too bad! And his breaststroke, while still not flashy, is greatly improved.

We continue to develop Michael as a complete swimmer. That means some emphasis on the distance freestyle. On Halloween, he whipped off a 5,000 free for time in a 46:34. That's under a 9:20 per 1,000 average. I was impressed with that. In fact, it is probably the most impressive thing he's done, and it might be one of the most impressive things he ever does. That's the kind of thing I'm not sure you can ever replicate, but it's neat to give him some confidence, particularly since he has to swim against some of the super distance guys.

This is the third year we have approached the training cycle from a yearly perspective. It's not our style at NBAC to talk about the results of success. We are always interested in the process. Michael didn't understand the scope of it until his breakout spring nationals performance in Seattle in 2000 when he went from a 2:04.68 to 1:59-flat and set a 15-16 NAG record in the 200 meter fly. After that, the secret was out. [9]

Michael Phelps was not only told he had a stroke that would set a world record one day, but he needed to prepare himself by doing that stroke in practice. Yes, over and over, lap after lap, though at times mundane. Simple disciplinary actions, perfected over time, brought him Olympic excellence. Additionally, he was instructed on the need to condition himself like he did as a child, by strengthening the connection in his mind. Phelps learned that what happens on a daily basis would affect what happens in the championship. It was imperative to maintain that intensity. So many get caught up in the results, and they forget about the activity necessary to produce those results.

Phelps appearance at the 2008 Olympics had much to do with his preparedness and his commitment. It has become known that his training intensified, leading up to this moment. Many had never heard of Phelps until his Olympic brilliance as he shocked the world by his

performances.

When it comes down to winning the championship, persistence is a known requirement. Yet, if you fail to prepare, you've prepared to fail. I recount the preparedness of one of the greatest failures in his preparedness fueled his determination. He was quoted as saying,

> "Give me six hours to chop down a tree and I'll spend the first four sharpening the axe."

> He failed in business in 1831, he was defeated for the legislature in '32, he was elected to the legislature in '34, his sweetheart died in '35, he had a nervous breakdown in '36, he was defeated for Speaker in '38, he was defeated for elector in '40, he was defeated for Congress in '43, he was elected to Congress in '48, he was defeated for the Senate in '50, and he was defeated for Vice President in '56 and for the Senate in '58. But in 1860, he was elected President of the United States.[10]

> His numerous failures prepared him to holding the highest office in our nation. *As President, he built the Republican Party into a strong national organization. Further, he rallied most of the northern Democrats to the Union cause. On*

*January 1, 1863, he issued the Emancipation Proclamation that declared forever free those slaves within the Confederacy.*11

Being prepared is a requirement for anyone attempting to win in any chosen endeavor.

We find that failure contributes greatly to one's success. Michael Jordan, the greatest player to ever play the game of basketball addressed failing this way,

> *"I've missed more than 9,000 shots in my career, I've lost almost 300 games. Twenty six times I've been trusted to take the game winning shot and missed. I have failed over and over and over in my life. And that's why I succeed!"* 8

When we think of Michael Jordan, we remember him as "Air Jordan" with these stats: Six-time NBA champion (1991-93, 1996-98); MVP (1988, '91, '92, '96, '98); 10-time All-NBA First Team (1987-93, 1996-98) etc. Memories of his failures aren't foremost on our minds we just remember his achievements. For most of us we can still see him with his tongue hanging out as he took the ball to the hoop.

In grade school Albert Einstein was a very unimpressive student. So much that the when his dad asked the headmaster what profession his young son should pursue, the headmaster replied,

> "It doesn't matter, because he will never make success in anything."[9]

The rest is historic. Einstein became one of the greatest physicists of the 20th century. His persistence developed in him the natural gifts of genius.

She was referred to as "Moses" not only by the hundreds of slaves she helped to freedom, but also by the thousands of others she inspired. Because of her commitment to a cause Harriet Tubman became the most famous leader of the Underground Railroad to aid slaves escaping the Free states or Canada.

Her first expedition took place in 1851, when she managed to thread her way through the backwoods to Baltimore and return to the North with her sister and her sister's children. From that time until the onset of the Civil War, she traveled to the South about 18 times and helped close to 300 slaves escape. In 1857, led her parents to freedom in Auburn, New York, and resided there.

Tubman was never caught and never lost a slave to the Southern militia. As her reputation grew, so too did the desire among Southerners to put a stop to her activities. Rewards for her capture once totaled about $40,000, a lot of money in those days. During the Civil War, Tubman served as a nurse, scout, and sometime-spy for the Union army, mainly in South Carolina. She also took part in a military campaign that resulted in the rescue of 756 slaves and destroyed millions of dollars' worth of enemy property.

After the war, Tubman returned to Auburn and continued her involvement in social issues, including the women's rights movement. In 1908, she established a home in Auburn for elderly and indigent blacks that later became known as the Harriet Tubman Home. She died on March 10, 1913, at approximately age of 93.[10]

Tubman's passionate commitment of love for her people kept her going back until every slave was freed, regardless of the dangers involved.

The foregoing people are normal like you and me, though because of their own uniqueness they acquired their own unique brand of success. They were driven by an extra-ordinary determination to achieve their goals at all costs. Every opposition brought them closer to a "YES." They are adept at turning setbacks into comebacks.

"Nothing in the world can take the place of persistence. Talent will not. Nothing is more common than unsuccessful men with talent. Genius will not. Unrewarded genius is almost a proverb. Education will not. The world is full of educated derelicts. Persistence, determination and hard work make the difference."

— Calvin Coolidge

Persistence and determination! These special character traits ought to be embodied in the legacy we pass on to our children. It's a common trend that children tend to develop their relationship values from their parents. And those qualities they pass on to their future generations.

Here is an example of a tradition passed on. A new bride was one day making dinner for her husband. He noticed that she cut off both ends of the ham before putting it in the saucepan. He was taken aback and asked: Why such a move?

She responded that her mom always cut off the ends of the ham before cooking it, making it very delicious. One day while he was with her mother he asked her why she cut off the ends of the ham before cooking it.

She said she didn't know and that she saw her mom do it that way and it was delicious.

One day while with his wife's grandma he pried further about this ham cooking process. She said,

> *"I cut the ends off my ham because it was too big to fit in my small roasting pan. It has nothing to do with the taste and texture. I had to cut the ends out of the ham to get it to fit in my pan!"*

Just because someone else did it doesn't mean you should do it too because of tradition.

- Are you determined enough to make a difference?
- Will you create a new lineage of future champions with your values.

In the words of author Berton Braley:

> *"If you want a thing bad enough to go out and fight for it, to work day and night for it, to give up your time, and your sleep for it...if all that you dream and scheme is about it, and life seems useless and worthless without it...if you gladly sweat for it and fret for it and plan for it and lose all you terror of opposition for it...if you simply go after that thing you want with all of your capacity, strength and sagacity, faith, hope*

and confidence and stern pertinacity...if neither cold, poverty, famine, nor gout, sickness nor pain, of body and brain, can keep you away from the thing that you want...if dogged and grim you beseech it, with the help of God, you WILL get it!"[11]

Ask any successful person and they'll tell you that going through those walls towards their destiny took persistence, personality, passion, purpose and tapping into their potential in order to succeed. But once they broke through, their life like that of the beautiful butterfly emerging from the cocoon became enhanced.

How determined are you to become successful?

Notes

1. Marianne Williamson
   http://thinkexist.com/quotation/as_we_let_our_light_shine-
   we_consciously_give/341050.html

Introduction

1. Martin Luther King Jr.
   www.brainyquote.com/quotes/m/martinluth115056.html
2. Ibid. dontknowmuch.com/kids/mlk.html
3. Harland Stoncipher, Pre-Paid Legal Services.
   Inc.
4. Oprah Winfrey - Bio. www.answers.com/topic/oprah-
   winfrey

Chapter 1

1. William Danforth, *I Dare You* (St. Louis:
   American Youth Foundation, 1991), X.
1. Gerald Sindell, The Genius Machine, Novato,
   New World Library, 2009), 66
2. Warren Bennis, *On Becoming a Leader,* Inc.
   Ontario & New York, Addison-Wesley
   Publishing Company, 19890, 54
3. Mahatma Gandhi,
   thinkexist.com/quotation/be_the_change_you_w
   ant_to_see_in_the_world...

Chapter 2

1. Ken Blanchard, Leading At A Higher Level, Prentice Hall, New Jersey, 2007, 280

2. Rick Warren, The Purpose Driven Life, Grand Rapids, Zondervan, 2002), 319

3. Napoleon Hill, The Master Key To Riches/Your Magic Power To Be Rich, New York, Penguin Group, 2007), 363

4. James Allen, *As a Man Thinketh* (New York: Bantam Books Inc., 1982),

5. Julia Cameron, The Artist's Way, New York, Tatcher/Putman. 1992), 66

6. Ibid. 66

7. Mark Fisher/Marc Allen, How To Think Like A Millionaire, Novato, New World Library, 1997), 72 (Ibid)

8. Colonel Sanders. www.articlesbase.com/entrepreneurship-articles/colonel-sanders-story-of-entrepreneurship-1000394.html

9. J.Paul Getty. www.zeromillion.com/srs-j-paul-getty

Chapter 3

1. http://thinkexist.com/quotation/develop_a_pass ion_for_learning-if_you_do-you_will/10266.html

2. William Danforth, I Dare You, 5

3. BillGates'Bio.http://Inventors.about.com/od/gstartinventors /a./Bill_gates.html

4. Rosa Parks. Live My Passion, http://www.livemypassion.com/thoughts.htm

Chapter 4

1. John Maxwell, Becoming A Person Of Influence, Nashville, Thomas Nelson Publishers, 1997), 7
2. Brian Tracy, Millionaire Habits, Entrepreneur Press, 2006) xi, xii
3. Ibid. 196

Chapter 5

1. Skip Ross with Carole C. Carlson, *Say Yes to Your Potential* (Rockford, MI: Circle "A" Productions, 1983), 145, 146
2. Napoleon Hill, *Think and Grow Rich* (Chatsworth: Wilshire Book Company, 1999), 16
3. Martin Luther King Jr. UBR, Inc., The American, The New Business Magazine For People Who Think. -- http://www.people.ubr.com/
4. Abraham Lincoln, Alan Loy McGinnis, *Bringing Out the Best in People* (Minneapolis: Augsburg Publishing House, 1985), 76.
5. James Allen, 13
6. Malcolm Gladwell, Outliers, New York, Hachette Book Group, 2008), 18
7. Ibid. 18
8. Jordan.htpp://quotations.about.com/od/stillmorefamouspeople/a/michaeljoradan1.html
9. Einstein. http://www.essortment.com/all/biographyofein_rwdi.htm

10. The Civil War Society's "Encyclopedia of the Civil War" http://www.civilwarhome.com/tubmanbio.htm

11. Les Brown, Live Your Dreams, (New York. William Morrow & Company, Inc. 1992), 90

Available Services

Consulting and training sessions are available for groups as well as individuals.

For more information contact us via Email: teensuccess101@yahoo.com Or visit us at www. AndrewsLeadershipInternational.com

---

NEED A SPEAKER FOR YOUR EVENT?

Interested in having author John A. Andrews or another speaker from Andrews Leadership International to speak at your event about:

Leadership For EVER

- EMPOWERMENT
- VISION
- ENTERTAINMENT
- RELATIONSHIPS

Contact John A. Andrews at john@theteensuccess.com

ABOUT THE AUTHOR

National Bestselling Author John A. Andrews, screenwriter, producer, and author of several books, founded Teen Success in 2009. Its mission statement: To invigorate and stimulate teens to maximize their full potential, to be successful and become contributing citizens in the world. As an author of books on relationships, personal development, and vivid engaging stories, John is sought after as a motivational speaker to address success principles to young adults. John makes an impact in the lives of others because of his passion and commitment to make a difference in the world. Being

a father of three sons propels John even more in his desire to see teens succeed. Andrews, a divorced dad of three sons ages 14, 12 and 10, was born in the Islands of St. Vincent and the Grenadines. He grew up in a home of five sisters and three brothers. He recounts: "My parents were all about values: work hard, love God and never give up on dreams."

Self educated, John developed an interest for music. Although lacking the formal education he later put his knowledge and passion to good use, moonlighting as a disc jockey in New York. This paved the way for further exploration in the entertainment world. In 1994 John caught the acting bug. Leaving the Big Apple for Hollywood over a decade ago not only put several national TV commercials under his belt but helped him to find his niche.

His passion for writing started in 2002, when he was denied the rights to a 1970's classic film, which he so badly wanted to remake. In 2007, while etching two of his original screenplays, he published his first book "The 5 Steps to Changing Your Life" Currently he's publishing his fifteenth volume, while working on empowering teens worldwide.

In 2008 he not only published his second book but also wrote seven additional books that year, and produced the docu-drama based on his second book, Spread Some Love (Relationships 101).

See Imdb: http://www.imdb.com/title/tt0854677/.

UPCOMING RELEASES

MAXIMIZE YOUR POTENTIAL
SIGNIFICANCE 101

There are things you and I will accomplish in our lifetime that will not only astonish our relatives, friends, neighbors, co-workers but our enemies alike. It has been discovered that 90% of an iceberg rests beneath the surface. It may surprise you that each of us has at least 90% of our potential lying untapped. As human beings, we are known to only use that other 10% of our potential. Like going from good to great, the high achievers in life attain their highest heights by going from success to significance. At this level, their destiny not only embodies greatness but true significance; they add value to others. The well known axiom states: Success is adding value to self, significance is adding value to others. The successful achieves significance by tapping deeper and deeper into their unused capacity.

In my interaction with people of significance, I've discovered that they are not only specialists in their field. At one point in their lives they said yes to their potential. As visionaries, they continue to empower others to maximize their God given potential. They realize that they don't have a thousand years to live, so they do all they can with their time, money and skills. They abhor going to their graves with their music leashed.

You too can join the significant by simply saying yes to your God given potential.

JUNK IN THE TRUNK

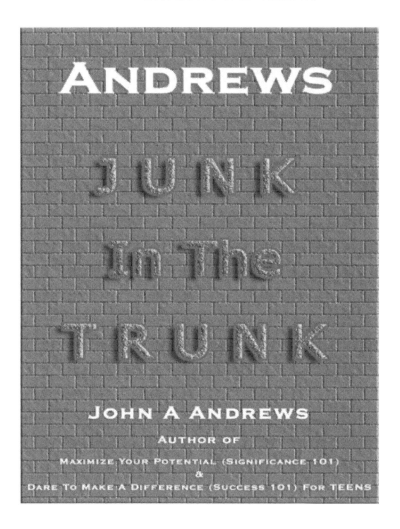

ANDREWS

JUNK

In The

TRUNK

JOHN A ANDREWS

AUTHOR OF

MAXIMIZE YOUR POTENTIAL (SIGNIFICANCE 101)
&
DARE TO MAKE A DIFFERENCE (SUCCESS 101) FOR TEENS

So many people spend a lifetime, looking in their rearview mirror. Their eyes, are focused on all that trash they carry around in the trunk.

This book tells you how to focus on the road, while you get rid of the junk in the trunk.

"QUOTES" UNLIMITED VOL. 2

ANDREWS

John A. Andrews

National Bestselling Author of

RUDE BUAY ... THE UNSTOPPABLE

Quotes from my treasury, and 101 other Quotes
Which Inspired Me.

When The Dust Settles – A True Hollywood Story

In life there are movers, shakers and detonators. Men who would not be denied as to their rightful place in society; they have what some may call "iron in their blood" and are driven by that steel-like will not-be - denied quality!

Coming to Hollywood is a dream cherished by almost every artist from the "wanna –be" to the "going to be". Yet making it here takes more than a desire but a will not be denied adventure - swimming up-stream. In this volume National Bestselling author John A. Andrews shares his challenging Hollywood Story.

Fasten your seatbelt and get ready for this journey as he takes you on his ride of a decade

RELEASES

"QUOTES" Unlimited.

Quotes from my treasury and 101 Quotes
Which Inspired Me.

*"If we think with a mindset of giving, we entertain abun-dance,
and if we think with an attitude of withholding, we invite lack. As
the source gives to the stream so ought the stream to impart to the
ocean."*

_ *John A. Andrews*

THE 5 STEPS TO CHANGING YOUR LIFE

"THE 5 STEPS TO CHANGING YOUR LIFE" In this book, John A. Andrews takes you on a journey from the inside out, extracting insights from his own life and great inspirational literature, most of them written several decades before he was born – delivering nugget after nugget of wisdom - essential for changing your life as well as impacting your world. So many embark upon the task of revolutionizing their home, their church and their world but never start with the "self." Everything you see on the outside first came from within. Real change is an "inside job." Learn the five fundamental steps necessary and pass it on to others.

"SPREAD SOME LOVE - Relationships 101"

SPREAD SOME LOVE (Relationships 101) was born out of his failed marriage which ended after 13 years in 2000. Since then John has not only read dozens of books on relation-ships but has associated with several experts on this subject, including Pastors Philip and Holly Wagner, whose marriage is now entering its 24th year. As an entrepreneur and sought after coach, Mr. Andrews believes that marriages should last forever and states: "If a person isn't willing to work on him or herself they should stay out of the falling in love business; the world is full of too many abandoned relationships and broken hearts."

TOTAL COMMITMENT –
THE MINDSET OF CHAMPIONS

By National Bestselling Author of Rude Buay ... The Unstoppable

TOTAL COMMITMENT
The Mindset of Champions

JOHN A. ANDREWS

Action is a doing word! Once you acquire this habit, others have no choice but to step aside for you. You are now a crusader, and the world always seems to make way for the person who knows where he or she is going.

HOW I WROTE 8 BOOKS IN ONE YEAR

How I Wrote 8 Books In One Year

JOHN A. ANDREWS

A

Author of
TOTAL COMMITMENT
The Mindset Of Champions

Writing my first book did not only cause me tap into my unused potential, but brought me off the sidelines and into the game. I decided that no one was going to outwork me. Since I had never taken a typing class, I was not adept at using the computer's keyboard. My word per minute was about a few words a minute. Someone once said: When the dream is big enough the facts don't count. In the summer of 2008, I wrote, published, and released Spread Some Love (Relationships 101).

It's my belief that if my thoughts can produce it, it can be written.

THE FORCESUM

THE FORCESUM
Total Empowerment For Women

Authors
Dee Petrov
Tia Thomas
Kathy Green
&
Dorensa Emanuel – Roberts
Foreword by National Bestselling Author-**John A. Andrews**

CONTACT INFORMATION

For more information about *JOHN A. ANDREWS*, to book speaking engagements, sign up for his mailings, purchase his books and to learn more about other BOOKS THAT WILL ENHANCE YOUR LIFE ™, visit his website at:

www. Theteensuccess.com
EMAIL
john@theteensuccess.com
or

Contact John at:

BOOKS THAT WILL ENHANCE YOUR LIFE™
www.booksthatwillenhanceyourlife.com

Made in the USA
Middletown, DE
25 October 2023

41302642R00085